W9-AJM-511

WORD BIRD
BUILDS A CITY

by Jane Belk Moncure
illustrated by Vera Gohman

THE CHILD'S WORLD

Library of Congress Cataloging in Publication Data

Moncure, Jane Belk.
  Word Bird builds a city.

  (Word Birds for early birds)
  Summary: Word Bird uses his blocks to build a
city complete with an airport, zoo, roads, and
neighborhoods.
  [1. Birds—Fiction. 2. Play—Fiction. 3. Vocabu-
lary] I. Gohman, Vera Kennedy, 1922-   , ill.
II. Title. III. Series: Moncure, Jane Belk. Word
Birds for early birds.
PZ7.M739Wn 1983   [E]   83-15257
ISBN 0-89565-257-9

WORD BIRD
BUILDS A CITY

One day Word Bird said, "I will build a city.

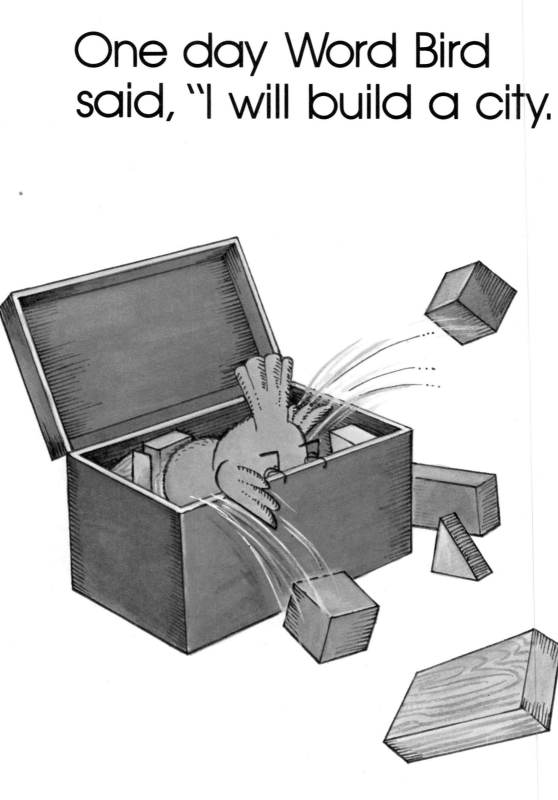

I need blocks...
lots of blocks."

First Word Bird
built roads...

lots of
roads.

What goes on roads?

Trucks,

cars,

buses,

motorbikes.

What else?

Then Word Bird built houses...

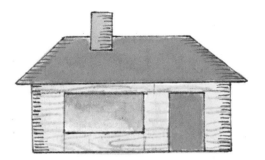

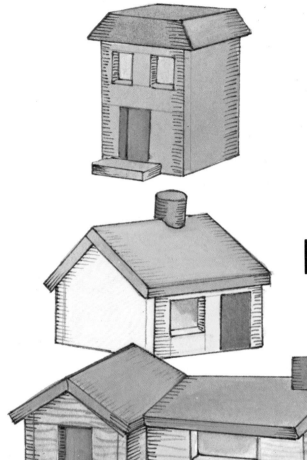

lots of houses.

What goes in a house?

A table,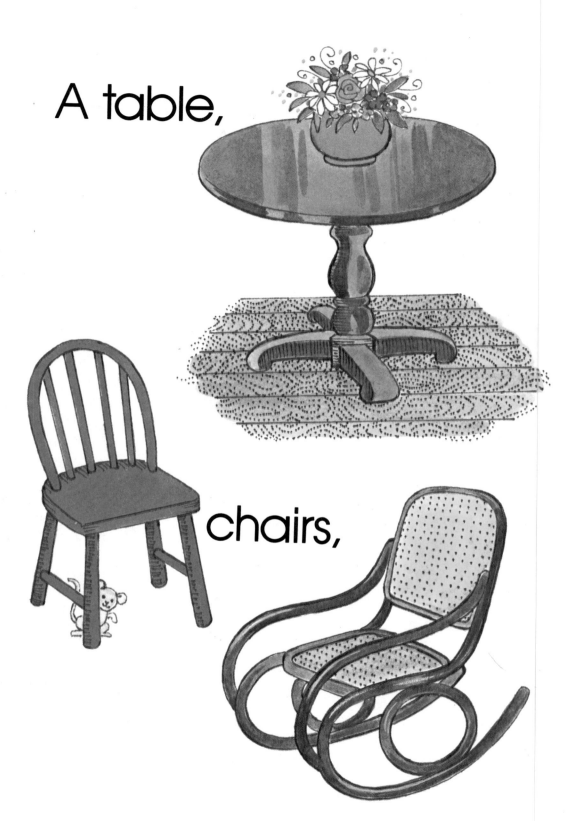

chairs,

a bed,

lamps.

What else?

Then Word Bird built a school.

What goes in a school?

A chalkboard,

blocks
road
school

desks,

books,

an easel,

paints,

crayons.

What else?

Then Word Bird
built stores...

lots of stores.

What goes in stores?

Cakes,

cookies,

bread,

toys,

ice cream,

 cereal,

watermelon,

pizza,

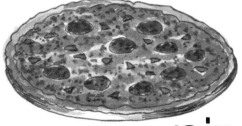

pets.

What else?

Next Word Bird built
a zoo.

What animals live
in a zoo?

A lion,

a monkey,

an elephant,

a giraffe,

a zebra.

What others?

Then Word Bird built
an airport.

BIRD CITY AIRPORT

What do airports have?

Passengers,

luggage,

jet planes,

runways.

When Papa came home, Word Bird said, "I built a city with blocks...

lots of
blocks."

You can read these  words.

blocks

road

house

school

store

zoo

airport

car

bed

desk

monkey

zebra

jet plane

What can you build?